THE WAR OF THE WORLDS

RETOLD BY PAULINE FRANCIS

Published by Evans Brothers Limited
2A Portman Mansions
Chiltern Street
London W1U 6NR

© Evans Brothers Limited 2005
This addition first published 2002
Original text by H G Wells.
Copyright by the Literary Executors of the Estate of H G Wells.

Printed in Malta

British Library Cataloguing in Publication data
Francis, Pauline
    The war of the worlds - (Fast track classics)
    1. Science fiction 2. Children's stories
    I. Title. II. Wells, H. G. (Herbert George), 1866-1946
    823.9'14 [J]

ISBN 0 23752405 8

THE WAR OF THE WORLDS

Introduction

Herbert George Wells was born in Kent, England, in 1866. His father owned a small shop and his mother was a lady's maid. Wells left school at the age of fourteen, but when he was eighteen years old, he won a scholarship to study science at London University.

By the time he was in his early thirties, Wells had already written the science-fiction novels that made him famous: *The Time Machine* (1895), *The Invisible Man* (1897) and *The War of the Worlds* (1898).

On 30 October, 1938 (Hallowe'en), *The War of the Worlds* was performed as a play on the radio in America. It included many announcements that the Martians had invaded America. Unfortunately, some people missed the first announcement which explained that this was only a play. There was great panic, especially around New York, as people tried to escape.

For the last forty years of his life, H.G. Wells was a world-famous writer. He wrote about forty novels and almost thirty non-fiction books, including the well-known *A Short History of the World*. H.G. Wells died in 1946.

CHAPTER ONE

The first falling star

"Heard about the dead men from Mars, sir?" the newspaper boy asked me early one Friday morning as I stood at the garden gate.

"What do you mean?" I asked in surprise.

"They landed in a big metal cylinder this morning, sir, near the sand-pits on Horsell

Common," he told me. "It's set all the heather on fire."

"How do you know all this?" I asked.

"That astronomer friend of yours, Mr Ogilvy, went to look," the boy answered. "He thinks there might be people trapped inside and he's gone for help."

Horsell Common was about two miles from my house on Maybury Hill, near the town of Woking. I decided to go there straight away. As I walked along, I thought back to the nights when I had looked at Mars through Ogilvy's telescope. Strange jets of gas erupted from the planet's surface, ten nights in a row.

"Meteorites!" Ogilvy exclaimed.

"There might be men on Mars trying to signal to us," I suggested. But Ogilvy just laughed.

I reached the sand-dunes on the common and stared in amazement. There was a huge cylinder almost completely buried in a hole about thirty yards in diameter, just as the boy had said. Fifteen or twenty people stood around and some boys were throwing stones at it.

I climbed down into the hole and looked carefully at the cylinder.

"I've never seen a metal like this before," I thought. "I am sure it has come from Mars, in spite of what Ogilvy thinks. I shall wait here until he comes back to open it."

I waited until eleven o'clock, but nobody came. I walked back home and tried to work in my study, but I could not concentrate. And when I saw the headline in the early evening newspaper – A MESSAGE RECEIVED FROM MARS – I decided to go back to the common. There was now a large crowd around the pit. Some people had come on bicycles from the villages, and others by train to the nearby railway station at Woking.

It was a wonderful June day, not a cloud in the sky, not a breath of wind. The fires in the heather had gone out, but the ground was black as far as I could see. Smoke still drifted into the air. My friend, Ogilvy, and other astronomers were down in the pit with spades and pickaxes. They had already dug out one end of the cylinder, but they could not unscrew the top.

I went home for tea and did not return to Horsell Common until the sun was setting. By then, almost two hundred people were standing around, getting in the way. A young man, a shop assistant I knew, was even standing on top of the cylinder.

"Look! There is somebody inside!" Ogilvy shouted, "they're unscrewing the top now!"

We all leaned over the pit, excited at what we might see. Suddenly, the head of the cylinder fell off with a loud clatter. I think we all expected to see a man come out. Nothing happened. Then I saw something move in the shadowy darkness of the cylinder, and I caught sight of two shining discs – like eyes. As I stared in surprise, something like a little grey snake wriggled in the air towards me – and then another!

I shivered suddenly.

The woman behind me gave a loud shriek. I turned and saw the looks of horror on the faces next to me. I looked at the cylinder again. More writhing tentacles were coming from it. I stood there, terrified. Then a big, greyish shape, about the size of a bear, rose slowly out of the cylinder, glistening in the light like wet leather. Two large dark eyes stared at me. Under these eyes, a v-shaped, lipless mouth dripped saliva. There was no chin. The creature's oily brown skin throbbed and it moved its tentacles all the time.

It terrified and disgusted me.

Suddenly, the monster fell into the pit with a loud thud. It gave a strange cry, then another creature appeared at the opening of the cylinder. I turned and ran away. But as I ran, I turned to look again and again. I could not take my eyes off those monsters. I reached the safety of some pine trees about a hundred yards away, and hid amongst them.

From there, I stared at the disgusting creatures. As I watched them, I saw the head and shoulders of the shop assistant at the edge of the pit, trying desperately to climb out. But he slipped back into the pit and I heard a faint shriek.

I could not move after that. I stood, knee-deep in the heather, staring for a long time at the mound of earth that hid the Martians. Twilight fell as more and more people arrived. I decided to move forward a little. I caught sight of a group of men walking towards the pit, carrying a white flag.

As the men came nearer, there was a sudden flash of light and greenish smoke rose out of the pit. I heard a hissing sound, which became a loud drone, then a round shape appeared. A beam of light seemed to flicker from it. In that blinding flash of light, men fell burning to the ground and bushes caught fire. I heard the crackle of flames everywhere.

This flaming death – this invisible sword of heat – swept swiftly round the common, curving around the sand-pits like an invisible finger. The dark ground between me and the Martians smoked and crackled. I stood completely still, amazed and dazzled by the flashes of light. Then the shape sank back into the pit and the night became black and terrifying once more. Filled with fear, I stumbled away through the heather. I was afraid, not only of the Martians, but also of the dark and the stillness around me. Then I ran, weeping like a child.

That night, nearly forty people – including my friend Ogilvy – lay dead under the starlight, burned to ashes by the Martian Heat-Ray.

A few seconds after midnight, another greenish light fell into the pine woods to the north-west. This was the second cylinder.

CHAPTER TWO

The Martian tripods

I reached home, dazed and trembling, and told my wife what I had seen.

"The Martians have done a foolish thing," I said to my wife, "but I expect it was because they are mad with terror. Perhaps they did not expect to find living things on Earth. We needn't worry - if the worst comes to the worst, the army will kill them all."

The next day, Saturday, lives in my memory as a day of suspense. It was hot and muggy. I tried to go close to the common again, but there were soldiers everywhere. The Martians did not show themselves at all. They seemed busy in their pit, hammering and banging, and sending up streams of smoke. What were they doing?

"They seem very helpless in that pit of theirs," I thought, "and if we do fight them, it will not be a fair battle."

In the afternoon, I heard the thud of gunfire from the direction of the second cylinder.

"The army is trying to destroy the cylinder before it opens," I told my wife. "But they still haven't done anything about the first one."

At five o'clock in the afternoon, the army at last

brought a field-gun to the nearby village of Chobham to use against the first Martians on Horsell Common. An hour later, we heard gunfire. Immediately afterwards, the ground began to shake. I saw the tops of nearby trees burst into smoky red flames. The tower of the church next to them collapsed. Even one of our chimneys cracked. My wife and I stood amazed.

"We can't possibly stay here!" I gasped. "We are within range of the Martian Heat-Ray."

"But where can we go?" my wife asked in terror.

"To my cousin's house in Leatherhead!" I shouted above the noise. "It's only twelve miles away!"

I managed to borrow a horse and small carriage from the landlord of the local inn. As we were leaving, we were shocked to see that the trees below the house were burning, and some of the garden fences glowed red. Soon we were clear of the smoke and the noise and we were rushing down the other side of Maybury Hill towards Woking.

In front of us, it was quiet and the sun shone on the wheat fields at the side of the road. At the bottom of the hill I turned my head to look back at the hill-side. Thick black smoke and flames shot into the still air a long way towards the east and the west.

"The Martians are setting fire to everything within range of their Heat-Ray!" I thought.

The road was dotted with people running towards us. At first, I could hear the faint noise of a machine-gun and the cracking of rifles. Then there was silence.

"Don't worry," I told my wife, "the Martians cannot escape from their pit. They are too heavy. The gravity on Earth is much stronger than on Mars."

We reached Leatherhead at about nine o'clock in the evening. I rested the horse there for about an hour, then set off for home.

"Don't go," my wife begged me, "it's too dangerous."

"I must take the horse and carriage back," I reminded her. "I promised the landlord."

I did not tell her that I wanted to go back to Maybury Hill! I wanted to be there when the Martians were killed.

If only I had known what lay ahead, I would have stayed with her.

The night was very dark and hot when I set off. On the horizon, I saw a blood-red glow. At midnight, as I came closer to Maybury Hill, a flash of green light came through the clouds and fell into the field to my left.

"The third cylinder!" I gasped.

At the same time, a storm broke out around me. Flashes of lightning lit up the sky and the thunder crackled. Out of the corner of my eye, I saw something moving down Maybury Hill in the flickering light. In a flash like daylight, this object stood out clear and sharp and bright.

How can I describe it? A great machine perched on top of three metal legs, a walking tripod of glittering metal, higher than many houses. It trampled the pine trees, clattering like thunder as it walked, covering a

hundred yards with each step. Then it stopped in the field where the cylinder had just fallen. To my horror, a second tripod appeared, walking straight towards me. I tried to pull my horse round quickly, but my carriage turned over and flung me into a pool of water.

This tripod walked past me, howling "ALOO! ALOO!" so loudly that the noise drowned out the thunder. I looked up and saw long, glittering tentacles swinging from its strange body, and a mass of white metal on its back, like a gigantic basket. I noticed the metal hood at its top, moving from side to side as if it was looking around. Puffs of green smoke squirted from its joints as it moved along. In another minute, it had joined up with another tripod half a mile away.

I should have gone back to Leatherhead straight away; but I did not realise the full meaning of those striding, metallic monsters. I made my way slowly home. Storm water was pouring down Maybury Hill and I had difficulty in reaching the top. Close to my house, I fell over the body of a man. In the next flash of lightning, I saw that it was the landlord of the inn who had lent me his horse and carriage. His neck was broken.

I ran into my house and locked the door. Then I crouched at the foot of the staircase with my back to the wall, shivering violently.

CHAPTER THREE

Escape from the Martians

At last, I forced myself upstairs to my study, which overlooked Horsell Common. A red glare shone around the sand-pits and three huge black shapes moved busily backwards and forwards in the light. What were they doing?

A noise in the garden stopped my thoughts. I looked through the window and saw a soldier in my garden. I went downstairs, unlocked the door and let him in.

"What has happened?" I asked him.

"They wiped us out – simply wiped us out," he said over and over again.

Then he began to sob like a little boy.

"Where are the Martians now?" I asked.

"They started to crawl in the direction of the second cylinder," he said, "under cover of a metal shield. Then…then…"

"Then what?" I asked, anxious.

"The shield staggered up on metal legs and began to walk," he gasped.

"The walking-machine!" I said, "I saw it on the hill as I came back."

"I lay under a dead horse," he sobbed. "I was scared

out of my wits. The monster had a kind of arm, carrying a metal box. Green flashes came out of it. It just walked backwards and forwards, killing everything in its sight."

"The Heat-Ray," I whispered.

"It killed everything on Horsell Common," he told me, "but it saved Woking until the last. The town's just a heap of burning ruins now."

The soldier put his head in his hands.

"There's hardly anybody alive in Woking," he cried. "One of the Martian giants ran after a man and picked him up with his tentacles. Then he knocked his head against the trunk of a pine tree."

We ate in the dark, afraid of attracting the Martians' attention. Afterwards, we went upstairs to my study and looked out of the window. In one night, the valley below us had become a valley of ashes. The flames had died down, but smoke still rose from the ruins of shattered houses. Blackened trees, hidden by the night, now stood out as dawn broke.

And shining with the light of the rising sun, three metallic giants now stood in the pit, their hooded heads rotating as they looked at the destruction they had caused.

"I'll fetch my wife from Leatherhead," I said. "We'll go to France." I paused. "But I can't go back the way I came. There's a third cylinder on that road."

"Go north, towards London then," the soldier said. "You can cut back down to Leatherhead. I'm going back to my regiment in London. We can go together."

We packed food and drink and walked north, through the town of Weybridge, to the River Thames. Here we found people trying to get away in boats across the river. Everything was quiet until the sound of gunfire drifted across the fields from the town of Chertsey.

At first, we could only see meadows, and cows and trees in the warm sunlight. Then, suddenly, we saw a puff of smoke far away up the river. The ground trembled and a loud explosion filled the air.

"Here they are!" a man shouted. "Over there! Look!"

Quickly, one after the other, five Martian tripods appeared over the treetops, striding across the meadows towards Chertsey. Their metal bodies glittered in the sun as they walked. One of the monsters lifted up a metal box high into the air. I held my breath. It was the ghostly and terrible Heat-Ray that I had seen on Friday night.

The monster destroyed Chertsey. There was no screaming from the crowd – only silence. But a few minutes later, people jumped into the river and tried to swim across. The rush of people knocked me over, and in the confusion, I lost sight of the soldier. I could think only of that terrible burning Heat-Ray and I crouched under the water.

One of the monsters stood right over me, holding up the Heat-Ray, but it was not looking down at the river. I raised my head above the water. As I looked, there was a burst of gunfire from the trees near the village of Shepperton. A shell exploded right in the face of the tripod above me. Its hood split into a dozen fragments of red flesh and glittering metal. It wobbled, then managed to carry on walking. But without a Martian to guide it, it smashed through Shepperton village and collapsed into the river.

As the Martian's Heat-Ray hit the water, it sent up a huge wave of steam which came sweeping along the river. People screamed and shouted as they were caught in the scalding water. The other Martians came to the spot immediately and set off their Heat-Rays. The noise was deafening – the clanking of the Martians, the crash of falling houses, the thud of trees, the crackling and roaring of fire. Their Heat-Rays flickered up and down the path by the river, only fifty yards from where I was hiding.

A moment later, the huge wave of boiling water reached me. I screamed in agony. I staggered from the hissing water and fell to the ground in full view of a Martian.

I waited for death.

CHAPTER FOUR

To London

I escaped by a miracle. The monster and his fellow Martians were too busy lifting the body of the dead Martian to see me. Their huge feet just missed me as they strode back towards Horsell Common.

As soon as it was safe, I walked on. I found a small boat near the river, and I decided to use it to get away from the fire and the smoke of burning Weybridge. There were no oars and I had to paddle painfully with my scalded hands.

"If the tripods come back, the water is my best chance of escape," I told myself.

At about five o'clock in the evening, I landed on the Middlesex bank of the River Thames. I fell asleep in the long grass by the river, then walked on. I stopped to sleep again. When I woke up, I saw a man dressed in curate's clothing sitting next to me, gazing up at the sky with large pale blue eyes. He must have found me a strange sight – my face and body blackened by smoke, and my scalded skin.

"Have you any water?" I asked.

He shook his head.

"What does it mean?" he said. "What do these things mean? What sins have we done? Fire, earthquake, death! Everything gone – everything destroyed. Our church in Weybridge! We rebuilt it only three years ago. Gone! Why?"

"You must keep calm," I said. "There is still hope."

"This is the beginning of the end," he whined. "The end!"

"Be a man!" I said. "What good is your religion if it collapses in time of trouble?"

I paused.

"The Martians will be coming this way again," I said at last. "We must carry on northwards to London."

At about eight o'clock that evening, we heard the sound of fighting in the distance, around Weybridge as we moved slowly northward. Suddenly, we saw three enormous shapes behind us, black against the western sky. It was the Martians, walking in a line, about a mile apart. They communicated with each other by giving high-pitched howls. The curate started running.

"You can't run away from a Martian!" I shouted. "Hide in the ditch!"

We could see other Martians now, in the distance.

"They're standing in the shape of a crescent," I whispered to the curate. "They must be guarding all their cylinders. Do they know there are soldiers everywhere?"

I stared at the looming monsters and waited. Suddenly, the army started to fire. The Martian nearest me was carrying a thick black tube. Now he pointed it towards the guns. It made such a loud noise that the ground trembled. But there was no smoke, no fire. The guns stopped and there was a long silence.

"What happened?" the curate asked.

"I don't know," I told him. "They didn't use the Heat-Ray. But they have silenced the guns again. The army doesn't stand a chance against them."

The Martian was now moving eastward along the river bank, disappearing slowly into the darkness. We decided to climb a hill to see what was happening. From the top, we could see a strange dark hill near the town of Sunbury, then another across the river. These hill-like shapes grew lower and broader as we watched.

I later learned the meaning of these strange hills in the twilight. Each Martian had sent a tube of thick, inky gas towards the hidden guns. It slowly spread over the surrounding countryside, killing everyone who breathed it. The Martians spread this strange, deadly gas over all the country towards London, as men smoke out a wasp's nest.

By Sunday night, every army gun in the area had been destroyed. And on this night, the fourth cylinder fell to Earth.

The curate and I hid in an empty house to escape the black smoke. We stayed there all Sunday night, watching the deadly smoke drift closer and closer. By Monday morning, it had reached the road outside the house. How much longer could we survive?

As we waited, terrified, we wondered what was happening everywhere else.

CHAPTER FIVE

My brother's story

It was only later that my brother, who lives in London, told me about that Monday – the day of the great panic in London. This is his story, in his own words, as he told it to me afterwards…

On Sunday morning, I bought my morning newspaper and was alarmed to read an article entitled MARTIANS LAND IN SURREY. It read as follows:

"The Martians, who landed near Woking on Friday morning, have been frightened by a large crowd of people. They used a quick-firing gun and killed many of the sightseers.

But there is no need to worry! The Martians are too heavy to crawl out of their pit …"

I decided to go to Waterloo Station immediately and catch a train to Woking, to see if my brother was alright. But when I arrived, there were no trains because of an accident on the line. I went back home and did not worry too much until I read a later newspaper:

"About seven o' clock last night, the Martians came out of their cylinder. They have destroyed Woking Station and many people, including soldiers. No details are known.

The Martians seem to be moving towards London. There is great anxiety in West Surrey and people are escaping along the roads north to London."

I rushed back to Waterloo Station, but there were still no trains. Now I was very worried, but had to go home when the police closed the station. As I walked under one of the most peaceful and golden skies I had ever seen, I saw the newspaper boys calling across the streets:

"DREADFUL CATASTROPHE!"

"MARTIANS FIGHTING AT WEYBRIDGE!"

"LONDON IN DANGER!"

The evening newspaper sent a chill down my spine.

"...the Martians control huge machines nearly a hundred feet high. They move as fast as express trains, shooting beams of great heat.

The situation is serious but there is no need to panic. There are only twenty of them and millions of us. The army has killed one of these machines and the rest have gone back to Woking. The public will be warned if there is any great danger."

I walked along Oxford Street and saw that it was already full of refugees, all with a look of horror on their faces, and wondered if my brother was alive or dead. I went to bed and tried to sleep.

Early the next morning, Monday, I was woken up by the sound of banging on the door downstairs. I looked through my window and saw a policeman.

"They are coming!" he shouted. "The Martians are coming! They are destroying everything on the way! Escape while you can!"

It was the dawn of the great panic – the day when six million people started to move northwards out of London, away from the Martians. By midday, a Martian had been seen at Barnes, south of the river, and a cloud of black gas was creeping along the Thames. I decided to try to reach some friends in Essex. All the tired, dusty people around me on the road had one thing in common – there was fear and pain on their faces.

"Go on! Go on!" they cried to each other. "They are coming! Go on!"

The farmers tried to protect their cows and pigs and chickens from us, but they could not. We ate every living thing on the farms, and ripped every crop from the fields. And as we walked, we saw the green flash of a sixth star, then a seventh, falling over London.

I decided to walk on to the east coast and find a boat to take me to France. When I reached the sea, I was relieved to see that there were plenty of boats. Now that they could not travel up the Thames to London, they had come to the Essex coast.

At last, I managed to get onto a little steamer, which set sail not a moment too soon.

As we sailed out into the North Sea, I saw what I had been dreading ever since I had left London – a Martian, small and faint in the distance, striding along the muddy coast. The captain swore at the top of his voice with fear and anger. I stood, terrified, as this monster waded further and further into the water. Then another appeared, striding over stunted trees. Then another!

To our relief, there was a warship, the *Thunder Child*, out at sea. It sailed at full speed towards three Martians looming over the water. The nearest Martian fired a thick black gas in its direction, but the ship managed to sail clear. Another Martian raised his Heat-Ray. At that moment, the *Thunder Child* fired. The Martian reeled and staggered and fell over. Then the gun ship headed for the second Martian who lifted up his Heat-Ray. With a blinding flash, the *Thunder Child* fired again and the Martian toppled over into the sea.

How we all cheered, watching from the deck of the steamer! The coast grew fainter in the rays of the sinking sun. We were safe at last!

Suddenly, the captain cried out and pointed up into the deep twilight. I looked up. Something was rushing into the sky – something flat and broad and very large. It swept round in a huge curve, grew smaller, sank slowly and disappeared into the night. And as it flew, it poured down black smoke over the land.

CHAPTER SIX

The fifth cylinder

As these terrible events took place that Monday morning, the curate and I watched the black smoke curling closer. Then, suddenly, at about midday, a Martian came across the fields and sprayed the smoke with a jet of steam that hissed against the walls of the house. The smoke died down at once.

"We can escape now!" I told the curate.

"But we are safe here," he repeated, "safe here."

I packed some food and drink and left him there. But at the very last minute, he came with me. We set off along the blackened road for the small town of Sunbury. There were twisted dead bodies everywhere, horses as well as men, all covered with black dust. We passed by Hampton Court, then Twickenham, and crossed Richmond Bridge at about eight o'clock that evening. The town of Richmond was in flames.

Further on, we saw people running towards us. I looked up. Over the tops of the houses, not more than a hundred yards from us, loomed a Martian tripod.

"If it looks down, we are dead!" I shouted.

We crept into a garden shed. The curate crouched in a corner, weeping silently, and refusing to go outside again. I set off again at dusk and he followed me. How foolish I was! There were Martians all around us. One of them chased some people across the fields, picked them up and dropped them into the metal basket on its back.

I watched, terrified.

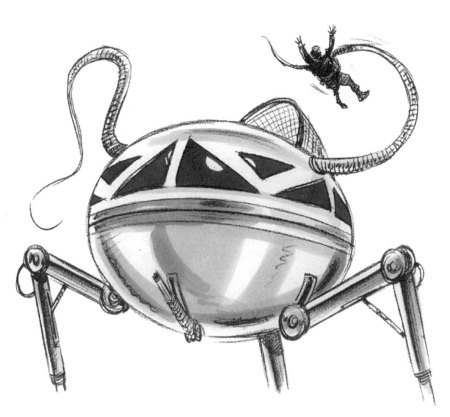

"What are they going to do with them?" I asked myself. "Why aren't they killing them?"

We hid in a ditch after that, until it was dark. Then, at about eleven o'clock, we set off again, keeping to the hedges and ditches. There seemed to be Martians all around us. At last, we came to the small town of Sheen.

"There's hardly any damage here," I whispered to the curate.

"Then let's look for food and drink," he replied. "I'm feeling faint."

We stopped at a white house, where we found a good store of food. We sat in the dark kitchen and ate.

"It can't be midnight yet," I said.

As I spoke, there was blinding flash of green light, followed by a loud thud and a clash of glass. Then falling bricks knocked me to the floor, unconscious. When I came round, the curate was leaning over me anxiously.

"Don't move," he whispered, "I think they are outside."

I listened. I could hear the rattle of metal.

"What is it?" I whispered.

"A Martian!" the curate answered, his voice trembling.

"I don't know what hit us," I said, "but it wasn't the Heat-Ray. Perhaps a fighting machine has fallen against the house. We'll have to stay here until daylight."

We hardly moved for three or four hours. As dawn broke, we saw the kitchen properly for the first time. Garden soil had broken the window and now lay everywhere. Most of the house had collapsed around us. As it grew lighter, we peeped outside through a gap in the wall. There, right in front of us, was a Martian. We crept to the darkness of the little scullery at the far end of the kitchen.

"The fifth cylinder," I whispered at last, "that Martian is guarding the fifth cylinder! It has struck this street and buried us under the ruins!"

"God have mercy upon us!" the curate whispered.

We sat in silence, surrounded by noise of the Martians – a metallic hammering, a violent hooting, a hissing. From time to time, loud thuds shook the house. The next evening, I crept to the hole again and peeped out. I could not believe the changes that had taken place since the day before. The cylinder lay in an enormous pit already much bigger than the one at Horsell Common. The front of the house had disappeared completely. Only the kitchen and the scullery remained.

I trembled violently as I realised our fate. We were hanging over the edge of a huge Martian pit!

CHAPTER SEVEN

Hiding from the Martians

We took it in turns to spy on the Martians. The cylinder was already open in the middle of the pit, but I hardly glanced at it. I stared in amazement at something else – an incredible machine like a metallic spider. It had five jointed legs - jointed levers moving up and down - and many tentacles on its body. With these, it was lifting metals rods and bars from the cylinder and placing them on the floor of the pit. But soon I realised that it was not a machine. Like the tripods, it was controlled by a Martian.

From my hiding-place, I could see the Martians more closely than before. I shivered with disgust as I looked at them. Their bodies were huge and round, about four feet in diameter, with a face in front. This face had no nose, just a fleshy beak. In the back of its head or body, was an ear. Grouped around its mouth were sixteen thin, whip-like tentacles, in two bunches of eight. They were trying to push themselves up on their hands, but it was difficult because of the stronger gravity on earth.

The creatures wore no clothes. There were no males or females. They seemed to be no more than enormous brains. When there was work to be done, the Martians simply controlled the right machine for the job. This is why their machines seemed almost alive.

The pit was never silent. A digging machine worked all the time, widening and deepening the pit. It whistled and piped as it worked, and sent jets of green smoke into the air.

"We shall have to stay here until they have finished their work," I whispered to the curate.

I groaned at the thought of being a prisoner with him any longer. He was beginning to drive me mad. He wept for hours on end. He was weak. He ate more than I did. He hardly slept. Sometimes, I lost my temper and hit him.

By the third or fourth day, a red creeper had begun to grow rapidly up the sides of the pit and its cactus-like branches hung like a fringe over our little peep-hole. At about this time, three more tripods arrived, bringing a strange machine with them. I watched this machine, fascinated. Two tentacles picked up lumps of clay. Another tentacle mixed it with a white powder, sending green smoke up into the air. Then a fourth tentacle lifted up a bar of shining white aluminium and placed it on the ground. Between sunset and starlight, this amazing machine made more than a hundred bars of aluminium, leaving a huge mound of blue dust at the side of the pit.

One evening, when the curate was watching through

the peep-hole, he stumbled away in terror. I took his place. At first, I could see no reason for his panic. It was twilight and the pit was lit up as usual by the green, flickering light. I could not see the Martians because they were now hidden by the mound of blue dust. I could only see a tripod standing across the corner of the pit, but I did not know if there was a Martian inside. Suddenly, I kept very still and listened carefully. I could hear human voices!

I crouched down and watched the tripod. As the green flames shot into the sky, I saw the oily gleam of the Martian's skin, and the brightness of his eyes. I heard a yell, and a long tentacle reached over the shoulder of the machine to the basket on its back and lifted something out. I saw by the green brightness that it was a man, struggling violently. He disappeared behind the blue-green mound. A loud shriek broke the silence, then the Martians hooted cheerfully. I put my hands over my ears and ran back to the scullery.

That night, I realised how terrible our position really was. But there was worse to come. On our third day in the pit, the Martians killed a boy. Then they fed on him - not on his flesh, but on his blood, which they sucked from a pipe directly into their own bodies.

I ran away from this terrible sight. I lost all hope. How could we ever escape these terrible monsters?

CHAPTER EIGHT

Alone!

On the sixth day, I went to the peep-hole as usual, but the curate did not follow me. When I went back to the scullery, he was drinking a bottle of wine. I snatched it from him and it broke on the floor.

"We must make the food and drink last," I whispered angrily.

But that afternoon, he tried to steal some food. From then on, we sat watching each other all the time. The curate wept and complained and talked noisily to himself. He had gone mad.

"Oh God!" he said over and over again. "We have sinned."

He babbled for two days.

"Shut up!" I cried, getting to my feet. "For God's sake, the Martians will hear us!"

"No!" he shouted, "I must speak! The word of God is upon me!"

He walked towards the kitchen.

"It has been too long!" he cried. "I must go outside!"

I was terrified that the Martians would discover us. I put out my hand and took a meat-chopper hanging on the wall and went after him. I had to stop him! I hit him on the back of the head with the handle and he fell to the floor. He lay still.

Suddenly, I heard a clattering noise outside and the room went dark. There was the digging-machine right across the hole. Then, to my horror, I saw the large dark eyes of a Martian, peering into the kitchen. A long metallic tentacle came slowly through the hole. The monster was now two or three yards into the room, twisting and turning. I ran through the scullery to the coal cellar. Had the Martian seen me? What was it doing now?

I crept to the door and peeped out. The Martian was dragging the curate's body towards the opening. I crouched there, listened. The metallic jingle came back. I heard it coming nearer, right into the scullery, then scraping across the cellar door. Then it began to turn the door handle! I could hardly breathe as I watched the door slowly open.

In the darkness, I could see just one thing – something like an elephant's trunk – waving towards me. It was like a black worm, swaying backwards and forwards. It touched the heel of my boot. I bit my hand to stop myself screaming. Then it picked up a lump of coal and went back to the kitchen.

I heard it smashing bottles and rattling biscuit tins. Then there was silence. Had it gone? At last, I decided

that it had, but I dared not leave my hiding-place. I lay
the whole of the tenth day in the darkness, buried in the
coal. I did not even dare to crawl out to find a drink.

On the eleventh day, I came out. My heart sank as I
saw that every scrap of food had gone, but I found a little
rainwater by the sink. I slept on and off through two
more days. By this time, the light that came in through
the hole was no longer grey, but blood-red. On the
fourteenth day, I crept into the kitchen for the first time
and found that the red weed had grown right across the
peep-hole.

The next day, my fifteenth day as a prisoner, I heard a
strange noise in the kitchen – a snuffling and scratching.

My heart began to beat faster. I listened again. It sounded like a dog! I went quietly into the kitchen and saw a dog's nose pushing through the red weed.

"Ssh…good dog," I whispered. "Don't bark!"

I noticed how quiet it was outside. What were the Martians doing? Were they waiting out there for me? I lay next to the hole for a long time until I was brave enough to look out. I could hardly believe my eyes. The pit was completely empty.

I stepped slowly outside, trembling. I hesitated, then, with my heart beating violently, I climbed to the top of the pit in which I had been buried so long.

I hardly recognised the world I saw.

CHAPTER NINE

A strange world

When I had last seen this part of Sheen two weeks ago, it had been full of red and white houses, and shady streets. Now all the houses were rubble, and the red weed grew everywhere. I had expected to see Sheen in ruins, but I was looking at a landscape that I did not recognise – the landscape of another planet. I stood for a moment, stunned by what I saw, until hunger made me move on.

I set off through the red weed, sometimes buried up to my neck, and made my way through scarlet and crimson trees towards Kew. It was like walking through gigantic drops of blood. The river was choked with the weed. The bridge over the Thames at Putney was almost buried by it. Here the scenery changed. There were patches of complete rubble with houses in between which had not been touched, as if their owners had gone out for the day. All food had already been stolen from them. I had to eat some of the red weed and it had a sickly, metallic taste.

I looked down from the Putney Bridge and the sight of the blackened trees, the ruins and the red-tinged river filled me with terror. There was silence everywhere. No people, no Martians.

"Am I the last man alive here?" I wondered. "Are the Martians now destroying the rest of the country, or even Paris?"

I slept badly in a small inn. In the morning, I walked down to Wimbledon Common where there was no red weed. But I felt that somebody was watching me from the bushes. I turned round and saw a man with a knife.

"Stop!" he said. "This is my country. All this hill down to the river. There is only enough food for one person. Which way are you going?"

"I don't know," I told him. "I have been buried in the ruins of a house for two weeks. I've no wish to stop here. I'm going to find my wife in Leatherhead."

"I know you!" he said. "You live in Woking, don't you! It's only sixteen days since I saw you, but your hair has turned grey! So we both escaped the killing in Weybridge."

"You're the soldier who came into my garden!" I gasped.

We shook hands.

"Have you seen any Martians?" I asked.

"They've gone across to north London," he said. "The sky is alive with their lights at night. I haven't seen them here for five days. But the night before last, I saw something up in the air. I believe they've built a flying machine."

"If they can do that, they will go round the world," I said sadly. "Mankind is finished."

"And they keep on coming," he said. "Green stars were still falling until last week. I've counted ten so far."

"So that's what I saw through my friend's telescope!" I said, "I was watching the Martians leave their planet."

"It was never a real war," the soldier said sadly. "We're just like ants to them."

I nodded.

"When they've built all their machines, they'll start catching more of us, keeping us in cages, eating us," he carried on. "Or keeping us as pets. Perhaps training us to fight our fellow men."

"What is there to live for?" I asked.

"We have to go on living for the sake of mankind," the soldier said. "We can't die out! We must live underground and breed. We must save our knowledge. We must bury books to protect them. We will spy on the Martians and learn to fight them. Perhaps we can even capture a fighting-machine."

We talked like this all night. But as I watched dawn breaking over London, I decided to leave this strange man with his strange dreams. I wanted to see what was really happening in London before I went to find my wife.

CHAPTER TEN

The end of the war

I came at last to Fulham Road, in London, where bodies lay in the streets covered with black powder. The closer I came to the city centre, the greater the silence became. The silence of waiting was worse than the silence of the dead. At any moment, the Martians might strike again.

It was near South Kensington that I first heard the howling. It sounded like two notes, "Ulla..ulla…" over and over again. It grew louder as I walked north, sending great waves of sound down the sunlit road.

Why was I wandering alone in this city of the dead? I felt so lonely. Oxford Street, too, was filled with black powder and skeletons picked clean by the birds. The same howling rang in my ears… "Ulla…ulla…"

At last, I came to Regent's Park and saw, far away over the trees, the head of a Martian tripod. It did not move towards me, but stood howling. To my surprise, I was not afraid. I made my way further north, towards Primrose Hill. Far away, through a gap in the trees, I saw a second Martian, standing completely still. Suddenly, the howling stopped. As night began to fall. I could feel the silence around me. I imagined a thousand enemies waiting for me, and I hid until morning. Then, walking on again at dawn, I saw a third Martian, standing completely still.

"I will die now!" I cried.

I walked straight towards the Martian tripod. But as I came near, I saw a flock of birds circling around its hood. My heart started to pound and I ran up to the motionless monster. Out of the hood hung shreds of brown flesh, torn by the birds. The Martian inside was dead. But who had killed it?

I caught sight of huge mounds of earth on the crest of Primrose Hill.

"Another Martian pit!" I gasped.

Unafraid, I ran towards the mounds of earth and climbed to the top. I found myself standing on the edge of the biggest pit that the Martians had built. I looked down. To my surprise, there were overturned machines everywhere, now only glittering, harmless metal.

I looked up at a looming, motionless tripod and I saw shredded flesh dripping from its hood onto the hillside. Scattered around the pit were about fifty Martians, some in their overturned machines, some laid out in a row.

I stood staring down into the pit as the morning sun lit up the sky and I wept.

The Martians were dead.

As soon as the Martians fed from our people, they were doomed to die. The earth was saved just in time by our germs!

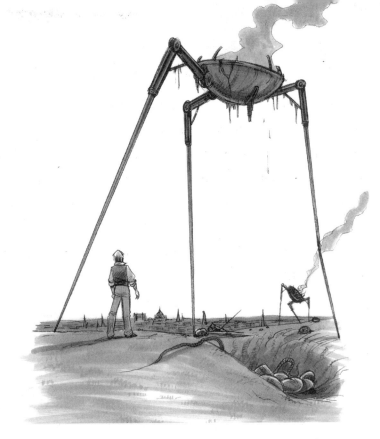

It is six years since these terrible events took place. My wife and my cousin were waiting for me when I went back to Maybury Hill. But all our lives have been changed for ever. Our planet has been robbed of its confidence in the future. What if the Martians attack us again?

But we have also learned that this planet is not just for us. Other people from other worlds might come here. And, if man is ever in danger of forgetting this, he should climb Primrose Hill – where a Martian tripod still stands.